JACK AND THE BEANSTALK

Joseph Jacobs

JACK
and the
BEANSTALK

ILLUSTRATED BY

MARGERY GILL

HENRY Z. WALCK, INC.
NEW YORK

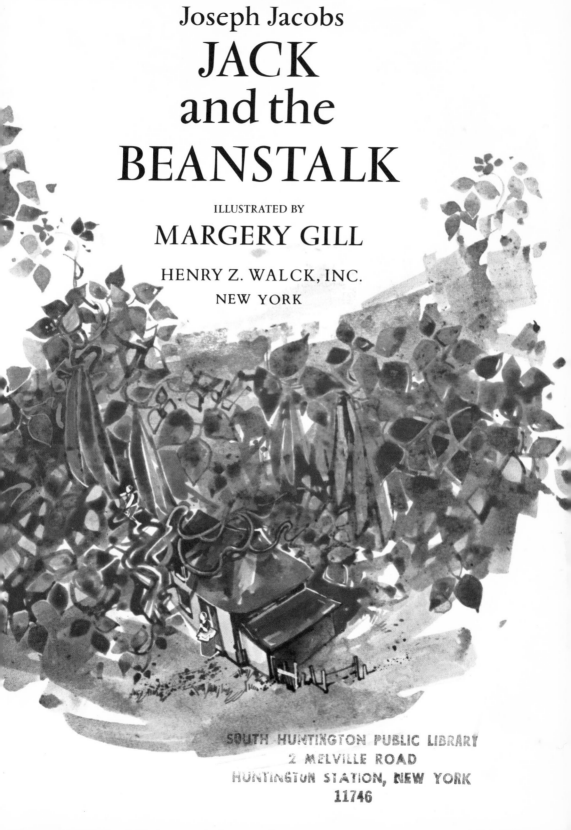

General Editor: Kathleen Lines

© Margery Gill 1975
ISBN: 0-8098-1221-5
Library of Congress Catalog Card Number: 74-5477
Printed in the United States of America

Library of Congress Cataloging in Publication Data

Jacobs, Joseph, 1854-1916.
   Jack and the beanstalk.
    (Walck fairy tales with historical notes)
   SUMMARY: Joseph Jacobs' version of the tale in
which a boy climbs to the top of a giant beanstalk
where he must use his quick wits to outsmart an ogre
and make his and his mother's fortune.
    [1. Fairy tales. 2. Folklore] I. Gill, Margery,
illus. II. Jack and the beanstalk.
PZ8.J19Jab5   398.2'1'0942[E]   74-5477
ISBN 0-8098-1221-5

There was once upon a time a poor widow who had
an only son named Jack, and a cow named Milky-
white. And all they had to live on was the milk the
cow gave every morning, which they carried to the
market and sold. But one morning Milky-white gave
no milk, and they didn't know what to do.

"What shall we do, what shall we do?" said the
widow, wringing her hands.

"Cheer up, mother, I'll go and get work some-
where," said Jack.

"We've tried that before, and nobody would take
you," said his mother; "we must sell Milky-white and
with the money start shop, or something."

"All right, mother," says Jack; "it's market-day today, and I'll soon sell Milky-white, and then we'll see what we can do."

So he took the cow's halter in his hand, and off he started. He hadn't gone far when he met a funny-looking old man, who said to him: "Good morning, Jack."

"Good morning to you," said Jack, and wondered how he knew his name.

"Well, Jack, and where are you off to?" said the man.

"I'm going to market to sell our cow here."

"Oh, you look the proper sort of chap to sell cows," said the man; "I wonder if you know how many beans make five."

"Two in each hand and one in your mouth," says Jack, as sharp as a needle.

"Right you are," says the man, "and here they are, the very beans themselves," he went on, pulling out of his pocket a number of strange-looking beans. "As you are so sharp," says he; "I don't mind doing a swop with you—your cow for these beans."

"Go along," says Jack; "wouldn't you like it?"

"Ah! you don't know what these beans are," said the man; "if you plant them overnight, by morning they grow right up to the sky."

"Really?" said Jack; "you don't say so."

"Yes, that is so, and if it doesn't turn out to be true you can have your cow back."

"Right," says Jack, and hands him over Milky-white's halter and pockets the beans.

Back goes Jack home, and as he hadn't gone very far it wasn't dusk by the time he got to his door.

"Back already, Jack?" said his mother; "I see you haven't got Milky-white, so you've sold her. How much did you get for her?"

"You'll never guess, mother," says Jack.

"No, you don't say so. Good boy! Five pounds, ten, fifteen, no, it can't be twenty."

"I told you you couldn't guess. What do you say to these beans; they're magical, plant them overnight and—"

"What!" says Jack's mother, "have you been such a fool, such a dolt, such an idiot, as to give away my Milky-white, the best milker in the parish, and prime beef to boot, for a set of paltry beans? Take that! Take that! Take that! And as for your precious beans here they go out of the window. And now off with you to bed. Not a sup shall you drink, and not a bit shall you swallow this very night."

So Jack went upstairs to his little room in the attic, and sad and sorry he was, to be sure, as much for his mother's sake, as for the loss of his supper.

At last he dropped off to sleep.

When he woke up, the room looked so funny. The sun was shining into part of it, and yet all the rest was quite dark and shady. So Jack jumped up and dressed himself and went to the window. And what do you think he saw? Why, the beans his mother had thrown out of the window into the garden had sprung up into a big beanstalk which went up and up and up till it reached the sky. So the man spoke truth after all.

The beanstalk grew up quite close past Jack's window, so all he had to do was to open it and give a jump on to the beanstalk which ran up just like a big ladder. So Jack climbed, and he climbed and he climbed and he climbed and he climbed and he climbed and he climbed till at last he reached the sky. And when he got there he found a long broad road going as straight as a dart. So he walked along and he walked along and he walked along till he came to a great big tall house, and on the doorstep there was a great big tall woman.

"Good morning, mum," says Jack, quite polite-like. "Could you be so kind as to give me some breakfast?" For he hadn't had anything to eat, you know, the night before and was as hungry as a hunter.

"It's breakfast you want, is it?" says the great big tall woman, "it's breakfast you'll be if you don't move off from here. My man is an ogre and there's nothing he likes better than boys broiled on toast. You'd better be moving on or he'll soon be coming."

"Oh! please, mum, do give me something to eat, mum. I've had nothing to eat since yesterday morning, really and truly, mum," says Jack. "I may as well be broiled as die of hunger."

Well, the ogre's wife was not half so bad after all. So she took Jack into the kitchen, and gave him a hunk of bread and cheese and a jug of milk. But Jack hadn't half finished these when thump! thump! thump! the whole house began to tremble with the noise of some-one coming.

"Goodness gracious me! It's my old man," said the ogre's wife, "what on earth shall I do? Come along quick and jump in here." And she bundled Jack into the oven just as the ogre came in.

He was a big one, to be sure. At his belt he had three calves strung up by the heels, and he unhooked them and threw them down on the table and said: "Here, wife, broil me a couple of these for breakfast. Ah! what's this I smell?

"Fee-fi-fo-fum,
  I smell the blood of an Englishman,
  Be he alive, or be he dead
  I'll have his bones to grind my bread."

"Nonsense, dear," said his wife, "you're dreaming. Or perhaps you smell the scraps of that little boy you liked so much for yesterday's dinner. Here, you go and have a wash and tidy up, and by the time you come back your breakfast'll be ready for you."

So off the ogre went, and Jack was just going to jump out of the oven and run away when the woman told him not. "Wait till he's asleep," says she; "he always has a doze after breakfast."

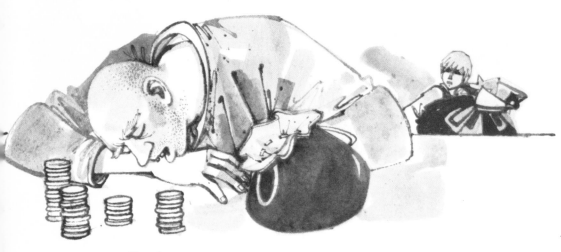

Well, the ogre had his breakfast, and after that he goes to a big chest and takes out of it a couple of bags of gold, and down he sits and counts till at last his head began to nod and he began to snore till the whole house shook again.

Then Jack crept out on tiptoe from his oven, and as he was passing the ogre he took one of the bags of gold under his arm, and off he pelters till he came to the beanstalk, and then he threw down the bag of gold, which, of course, fell into his mother's garden, and then he climbed down and climbed down till at last he got home and told his mother and showed her the gold and said: "Well, mother, wasn't I right about the beans? They are really magical, you see."

So they lived on the bag of gold for some time, but at last they came to the end of it, and Jack made up his mind to try his luck once more at the top of the bean-stalk. So one fine morning he rose up early, and got

on to the beanstalk, and he climbed and he climbed
and he climbed and he climbed and he climbed and he
climbed till at last he came out on to the road again
and up to the great big tall house he had been to before.
There, sure enough, was the great big tall woman
a-standing on the doorstep.

"Good morning, mum," says Jack, as bold as brass,
"could you be so good as to give me something to
eat?"

"Go away, my boy," said the big tall woman, "or
else my man will eat you up for breakfast. But aren't
you the youngster who came here once before? Do
you know, that very day my man missed one of his
bags of gold."

"That's strange, mum," said Jack, "I dare say I could tell you something about that, but I'm so hungry I can't speak till I've had something to eat."

Well, the big tall woman was so curious that she took him in and gave him something to eat. But he had scarcely begun munching it as slowly as he could when thump! thump! they heard the giant's footstep, and his wife hid Jack away in the oven.

All happened as it did before. In came the ogre as he did before, said: "Fe-fi-fo-fum", and had his breakfast off three broiled oxen. Then he said: "Wife, bring

me the hen that lays the golden eggs." So she brought it, and the ogre said: "Lay," and it laid an egg all of gold. And then the ogre began to nod his head, and to snore till the house shook.

Then Jack crept out of the oven on tiptoe and caught hold of the golden hen, and was off before you could say "Jack Robinson." But this time the hen gave a cackle which woke the ogre, and just as Jack got out of the house he heard him calling: "Wife, wife, what have you done with my golden hen?"

And the wife said: "Why, my dear?"

But that was all Jack heard, for he rushed off to the beanstalk and climbed down like a house on fire. And when he got home he showed his mother the wonderful hen, and said "Lay" to it; and it laid a golden egg every time he said "Lay."

Well, Jack was not content, and it wasn't very long before he determined to have another try at his luck up there at the top of the beanstalk. So one fine morning, he rose up early, and got on to the beanstalk, and he climbed and he climbed and he climbed and he climbed till he got to the top. But this time he knew better than to go straight to the ogre's house.

And when he got near it, he waited behind a bush till he saw the ogre's wife come out with a pail to get some water, and then he crept into the house and got into the copper. He hadn't been there long when he heard thump! thump! thump! as before, and in came the ogre and his wife.

"Fee-fi-fo-fum, I smell the blood of an Englishman," cried out the ogre. "I smell him, wife, I smell him."

"Do you, my dearie?" says the ogre's wife. "Then, if it's that little rogue that stole your gold and the hen that laid the golden eggs he's sure to have got into the oven." And they both rushed to the oven. But Jack wasn't there, luckily, and the ogre's wife said: "There you are again with your fee-fi-fo-fum. Why, of course, it's the boy you caught last night that I've just broiled for your breakfast. How forgetful I am, and how care-less you are not to know the difference between live and dead after all these years."

So the ogre sat down to the breakfast and ate it, but every now and then he would mutter: "Well, I could have sworn—" and he'd get up and search the larder and the cupboards and everything, only, luckily, he didn't think of the copper.

After breakfast was over, the ogre called out: "Wife, wife, bring me my golden harp." So she brought it and put it on the table before him. Then he said: "Sing!" and the golden harp sang most beautifully. And it went on singing till the ogre fell asleep, and commenced to snore like thunder.

Then Jack lifted up the copper-lid very quietly and got down like a mouse and crept on hands and knees till he came to the table, when up he crawled, caught hold of the golden harp and dashed with it towards the door. But the harp called out quite loud: "Master! Master!" and the ogre woke up just in time to see Jack running off with his harp.

Jack ran as fast as he could, and the ogre came rushing after, and would soon have caught him only Jack
had a start and dodged him a bit and knew where he
was going. When he got to the beanstalk the ogre was

not more than twenty yards away when suddenly he
saw Jack disappear like, and when he came to the end
of the road he saw Jack underneath climbing down
for dear life. Well, the ogre didn't like trusting himself
to such a ladder, and he stood and waited, so Jack got
another start. But just then the harp cried out: "Master!
Master!" and the ogre swung himself down on to the
beanstalk, which shook with his weight. Down climbs
Jack, and after him climbed the ogre. By this time
Jack had climbed down and climbed down and
climbed down till he was very nearly home. So he
called out: "Mother! Mother! bring me an axe, bring

me an axe." And his mother came rushing out with
the axe in her hand, but when she came to the beanstalk
she stood stock still with fright, for there she saw the
ogre with his legs just through the clouds.

But Jack jumped down and got hold of the axe and
gave a chop at the beanstalk which cut it half in two.
The ogre felt the beanstalk shake and quiver, so he
stopped to see what was the matter. Then Jack gave
another chop with the axe, and the beanstalk was cut

in two and began to topple over. Then the ogre fell
down and broke his crown, and the beanstalk came
toppling after.

Then Jack showed his mother his golden harp, and
what with showing that and selling the golden eggs,
Jack and his mother became very rich, and he married
a great princess, and they lived happy ever after.

JACK AND THE BEANSTALK

'Jack and the Beanstalk' was one of the twelve booklets which made up *The Home Treasury* of Felix Summerly, published intermittently between 1841 and 1849. They were as good versions as could be found among the chapbooks of traditional fairy tales, and marked the beginning of opposition to the theories of the serious-minded, pious American Samuel G. Goodrich, author of the popular 'Peter Parley' books, who, believing completely in the importance of his self-appointed mission, had denounced Halliwell, and all rhymes and fairy tales, saying that children should read 'facts not fiction'. Goodrich's factual and at the same time moral books were much in demand in England, so much so, and with every publisher wanting his share in satisfying the demand, that many were pirated and almost written expressly for England by false 'Peter Parleys'. Notwithstanding his imitators Goodrich was himself responsible for about one hundred and seventy books with sales reaching seven million. He was a formidable adversary, but so sure of his own worth that he had no fear of being misplaced and was hurt by unkind criticism.

But 'quality will out'. Of Peter Parley nothing remains, although the tales Felix Summerly saved and edited have been retold time after time, and even today hold their place as essentials in any collection of nursery tales.

Joseph Jacobs had the story of Jack and the Beanstalk told to him when a child in Australia, and that recollected version provides the text for this picture book edition.

There is not space enough here to discuss the variations in the texts of other editions, but if the story is read in, say for example—Lang's *Blue Fairy Book*, Warne's *Book of Nursery Tales*, Dent's *Fairy Tales of Long Ago*, and the retellings by Mrs Steel, Mrs Williams-Ellis and Sir Ernest Rhys a surprising number of differences will be found; that some chapbooks survived beyond their time accounts no doubt for differences not only in plot but in the tone of the tale itself. And since even in the few books mentioned some versions fairly bristle with moral injunctions it would seem that Peter Parley's fellow thinkers had laid 'improving' hands on an old text or told the old tale in a new way.

Jacobs' version is in perfect form for storytellers, simple in style (one might call it homely), and spontaneous but dramatic, with natural idiomatic conversation. The narrative is natural too, told in the words ordinary people might use, and there are light-hearted touches of humour. The two or three points in which it differs from accepted tradition, the giant's verse, and the 'golden' hen, with the final emphasis on 'riches' (the word is used only in one other version to my knowledge) add up to very little considering the outstanding excellence of the tale as Jacobs tells it.   KATHLEEN LINES